2030

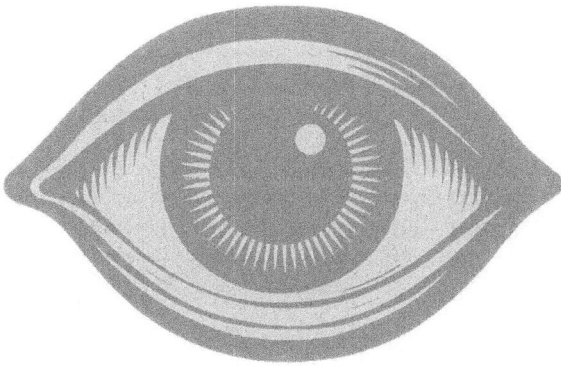

Mike Fairclough

Fisher King Publishing

2030

Print ISBN 978-1-916776-86-9
Ebook ISBN 978-1-916776-87-6

Published worldwide by Fisher King Publishing
fisherkingpublishing.co.uk

With my beautiful wife and warrior woman
Sundeep by my side we dedicate this book to
our inspiring children Tali, Iggy, Luna and Star
and to our precious granddaughter Alice.

Beyond our own family this dedication reaches
out to all children, all teenagers, and all young
people who will inherit the future.

To the parents who choose to stand with them,
to guide, protect and join the resistance, we
honour your courage too.

Do not allow the flaws of the adult
world to write your destiny.

Grasp it with courage.
Shape it with vision.
Claim it as your own.

Your time to rise is now.

Prologue

I want to speak to you directly, before the story begins.

When I was your age, the books we studied at school were dangerous in the best sense of the word. We read George Orwell's *Animal Farm* and *1984*. We read William Golding's *Lord of the Flies*. We were exposed to stories of mythological heroes - ordinary men and women who faced extraordinary challenges. These books didn't come with 'trigger warnings.' They weren't wrapped in cotton wool. They were meant to disturb, to challenge, to wake you up.

I grew up in a time when boys were boys and girls were girls. Our fathers, and our grandfathers before them, had fought in wars or been raised in the shadow of those who did. They taught us grit, resilience, and the courage to stand up when something was wrong.

We were also raised with pride in our British heritage. Our history, our culture, our traditions, and our flag were things to respect, not to be ashamed of. We learned that our nation had stood up against tyranny, twice, and paid the price in blood. We sang songs that carried our past. We flew the Union Jack as a symbol of unity, freedom, and identity.

Today, children and young people are told to see their history not as a source of pride or strength, but as a catalogue of guilt. They are taught that the victories of their ancestors were crimes, that courage was cruelty, and that sacrifice was oppression. They are urged to turn away from their heritage, to treat their own flag as a symbol of shame, and to believe that the culture which once defended freedom is now too offensive to exist.

Much of what shaped us has been stolen from you. Books that once inspired rebellion are now treated as dangerous objects. Classrooms have become indoctrination centres. Children are drilled to fear the weather, to doubt their own identity, to repeat slogans about 'inclusion' while real truth is erased. Men are called 'toxic' simply for being men. Women are told that men can be women and therefore women are redundant.

I spent many years as the headmaster of a school,

and almost thirty years teaching within the English education system. I am now the author of books, an editor, a ghostwriter, and a campaigner for freedom. I have lost count of the number of parents who have said to me, *Write something for our children, something that tells the truth.*

That is why I have written *2030*.

Make no mistake, this book is not pure fiction. It is a prophecy. If we do nothing, if we stay silent, if we accept every slogan and every fear they press upon us, then 2030 will not be a story. It will be your future. Adults may deny this, but the task of resistance will fall to the young. To you.

So read carefully. Remember what has been erased. And when the time comes for you to stand, take your decision with conviction and purpose. Because if you do not stand, nobody else will.

A Note on Style

As a headmaster, my approach to education was celebrated internationally. It was rooted in something called character education, a philosophy in which young people were expected to move beyond their comfort zones. I saw children thrive when they lit fires in sub-zero temperatures, fired shotguns with steady hands, camped under the stars, and faced personal challenges that demanded grit. Those experiences expanded them. They forged strength. They forged resilience.

This book has been written with the same spirit. You are about to enter a dystopian world. It is deliberately crafted to feel that way. The early chapters may feel like a grind, heavy, relentless. That is intentional. This is not TikTok with its quick dopamine hits, nor a Hollywood blockbuster that begins with explosions. This story asks for your focus, your stamina. The hardest journeys are the ones that change us most deeply.

And while the opening chapters set the weight of this world, know that the journey does not remain there. The path widens, the pace quickens, and what follows will reward your perseverance.

2030 is not an ordinary book. You will discover, as

you read, that you are not simply an observer. You are a participant. This story is rooted in truth. You, the reader, have the most important role to play.

So buckle up. Stay with me. Let us step together into 2030. Because until you realise you are sleepwalking into dystopia, you cannot begin to unlock the prison door.

And when that moment comes, you will discover just how powerful you truly are.

Chapter 1
The Digital Prison

George woke to silence. Not the silence of peace, but the heavy, engineered quiet of a world with no birdsong, no traffic, no laughter. The Council had found ways to mute even the dawn.

His room was the same as every other room, square walls, pale light, a bed without softness. A clock blinked on the wall, but its hands did not tick. Time was measured now in doses and data, not in minutes and hours.

He sat up slowly, pressing his palms against his eyes. The same dream again, a sound he could not place, a ripple of joy, a child's laugh that did not belong in this world. He tried to catch it, to hold it in his memory, but it slipped away like water through his fingers.

The World Safety Council called these fragments 'spikes.' Citizens were taught to report them immediately, to present themselves for correction. But George had learned to keep his silence. To carry the spike quietly. To let it burn like a secret fire.

Today would be no different. He would dress in the World Safety Council's uniform, walk the Council's streets, speak the Council's words. But deep inside, he carried something the injections and lessons had never erased. A trace of another life. A whisper that the world had once been more than this.

And the walls, though he did not yet know it, remembered too.

The Silence of Yesterday

The clock in George's flat did not tick.

Clocks that ticked had been deprecated as stress-positive devices. A tick suggested something counting down, not up, and the World Safety Council wished people to feel their days as open, ambient, un-threatening. It was the sort of kindness a citizen could drown in.

The morning Guidance slid across the wall like

weather, pastel colours, a face that was neither male nor female, neither old nor young. A neutral blur of humanity, pleasant and disposable.

"Good citizens practise Soft Speech at breakfast." The voice was a fog of vowels.

"Hard consonants are spikes. Spikes are violence. Violence is gone."

George sipped from his mug. On the base, his Digital ID pulsed green:

ATI: 87.3: Acceptable
Injection Record: 365/365: Compliant

The numbers were his life. Every newborn received one injection for every day of its first year, a perfect calendar of obedience. Three hundred and sixty-five needles pressed into flesh before memory began. The injections had to be updated with boosters, with individuals taking full responsibility for this important safety measure.

Every year after their birth, each citizen marked their Death Day, the official reminder that life was a state-owned lease. Length of term depended on compliance. Life extension was granted in twelve-month packages, never guaranteed.

George was different in one way only. He had been born in the old world. He had once had a childhood, a family, a history. But all of it had been cleared, updated, rewritten into state-approved memories when the transition came.

He was still a *he*, one of the last. Newborns were no longer boys or girls. They were raised as *they, their, them*, genderless, historyless, interchangeable. George's very pronoun marked him as a relic, though he carried the burden silently.

The coffee-substitute was brown, thin, and without flavour. That was deliberate. Food was not meant to tempt, only to fuel. He tried to taste what wasn't there and failed.

A thought surfaced, *spikes are useful things*. He dismissed it quickly. The walls had a way of remembering.

He dressed in slate compliance cloth, the kind that

never creased and never flattered, and left his unit.

Doors along the corridor sighed open and shut in rhythm. From one came the sound of vowels being practised, "Ah, aw, oh." From another came silence, which was safer still.

The Pod's perimeter arch gleamed the white of a dentist's smile. Two World Safety Council Auditors stood with HushWands hanging like canes. George extended his wrist. The scanner hummed, and his record appeared in the air:

Citizen: GEORGE
ATI: 87.3: Acceptable
Injection Total: 365/365: Compliant
Movement Quota: 00:17:42: Remaining

The Auditor glanced, expression neutral. George lowered his eyes in gratitude. Gratitude was safer than pride.

Behind him, another citizen's display flared red:

Injection Total: 363/365: Overdue

The gate announced in its soothing tone, "Corrective Care required." Two Auditors detached, taking the citizen away without fuss. The arch pulsed brighter, satisfied.

George walked on. Curiosity was dangerous. Pausing to watch was an indication of pre-emptive crime.

The World Safety Council headquarters occupied what had once been a department store. Escalators still moved the compliant up and the irrelevant down.

A mural spread across the atrium, citizens in neutral robes, holding hands in a circle, mouths blurred to ovals. A plaque beneath read:

HAPPINESS IS HARMONY.
HARMONY IS HAPPINESS.

On Floor 3, Heritage Feed, George sat at his station. His task was not to create or to record, but to erase.

The Council AI did the heavy lifting, analysing billions of words each day from the endless lattice of facial-recognition cameras. It listened for spikes, words spoken too sharply, tones too high, syllables bitten like teeth.

It also tracked movement, a step too fast, a gesture too broad, a breath drawn too deep. Each excess was a selfish act, depleting the planet of air.

The AI flagged. George confirmed. His human eyes gave flesh to the machine's suspicion.

A boy's voice rose too suddenly: spike.
A woman coughed twice in a row: excess.
A man turned his head too quickly, exhaling more carbon than allotted: wasteful.

Each was marked, recorded, and passed on for correction.

George pressed Submit. His ledger rose to 87.6. The screen warmed approvingly.

At mid-day, citizens assembled in the canteen. Nutrient paste steamed beige in bowls. On the wallscreens, the daily slogan repeated:

UP TO DATE IS UP TO SAFE. SAFE IS HAPPY. HAPPY IS UP TO DATE.

A Council Auditor named Parrott sat opposite, spoon raised like a preacher's staff.

"Good tidings!" Parrott chirped. "The Council is trialling a three hundred and sixty-sixth injection for leap years. Imagine the symmetry. No child left unprotected."

George stirred the paste.

"Conflict incidents fell another half-point this quarter," Parrott went on. "Injection ensures tranquillity. Soon dissent will vanish altogether."

George gave the smile that was safe.

"Compliance breeds kindness," Parrott declared. "And kindness is the highest form of thought."

George nodded, remembering the words erased last week: awkward, blunt, furious. He wondered how anyone could describe affection without them. He sealed the thought away before it showed.

After lunch, the auditorium filled. A Council Auditor demonstrated Correct Speech, vowels softened like soap, consonants rounded like balloons.

Citizens repeated:

"Happiness is harmony. Harmony is happiness."

George spoke along, his voice thin, obedient. He thought, just for a moment, that the words pressed against the walls like water on stone, leaving marks no one could see.

After work, when he returned to his flat, the Guidance whispered, "Up to date is up to safe. Safe is happy. Happy is up to date." The tickless clock hummed.

The Council promised equality. No one was allowed to be richer, hungrier, colder, or lonelier than anyone else. They promised freedom from want, freedom from hardship, freedom from pain.

To suffer was forbidden, because suffering caused spikes.

George lay still, eyes open to the ceiling. Tomorrow would be the same. Tomorrow always was.

George would be turning twenty years of age tomorrow. Birthdays continued to be the one date which was allowed recognition. But what he could remember from before this time was lost. This absence, to him, felt like a prison.

And yet, he wondered, could the very chains of this life become the key to unlock the door? Could the system's grip tighten so far that it cracked itself, allowing something buried to slip free?

The thought was not just a thought. It was a distant feeling, the kind that lives just beyond reach, like trying to remember a forgotten dream. A shape without detail. A warmth without source.

It pressed against him faintly, as though from another lifetime, or from someone else's memory leaking into his own.

Somewhere, far below the Pod, far beyond the Guidance, someone else was already asking the same question.

Chapter 2
The Walls Remember

The summons was not a message but an absence.

At 06:10 the morning Guidance failed to load for a few seconds. The living wall went blank, no pastel, no slogans, only the raw, patient plaster beneath. Then the feed resumed as if nothing had happened, a neutral face explaining how to soften a scolding into a 'care phrase.'

Most citizens would not even have noticed. They lived without memory. Since 2028, entire populations had been cleared, smoothed, and reset. They could not recall a yesterday that was not already approved, and so a three-second absence in a wall was as invisible as a bird flying in the dark.

But George noticed. He noticed because he still had fragments, feelings, really, like shadows of dreams that could never be fully remembered.

And he was not alone.

The Persistence of the Soul

No one knew exactly how it had begun. Perhaps it was a fault in the machinery of memory-clearing. Perhaps it was something deeper, something the World Safety Council had not accounted for, the persistence of the soul.

In this Godless society, engineered to worship only safety, a few citizens retained the spark, an ache, a flicker, the capacity to feel that something was missing.

They had found each other slowly. A glance too long in a corridor. A hesitation before repeating the slogans. A silence that spoke more than words. Small bands gathered, not because they knew what they were, but because they recognised in one another the same haunted incompleteness.

Among them was one who worked on the World Safety Council's AI system itself. That machine, the lattice of eyes and ears that turned billions into drones. It had been asked the wrong question. Or perhaps the right one. It had been tricked, hacked, persuaded into explaining what it was never meant to share. How walls could be made to speak.

The old world governments had known this for decades. Long before 2030, the elites had been listening to history itself. They had decoded the Colosseum, hearing Latin shouted across its stones, hearing the clash of gladiators' swords. They had pried secrets from the pyramids, listening to the breath of slaves and the commands of kings. They had unearthed secrets entombed in palaces and parliaments, crimes so old they no longer lived in paper but only in stone.

And with those revelations came leverage. Blackmail. Extortion. Every leader, every magnate, every priest, every king, they were all guilty of something. Client lists whispered through plaster. Secrets of the powerful replayed from ancient walls. It was not history as we had known it but as it truly was, and it was used as a weapon.

When the extortion was no longer enough, the knives came out. Murder followed, and then the tightening of the agenda, all to bury or control what had been revealed.

But there was something deeper still.

As the walls spoke, it became clear that the history citizens in the old world had been taught was itself a fabrication. The official stories of nations, of wars, of victories and defeats, much of it had been constructed, rewritten to protect those in power.

Words had been stolen. Technologies had been buried. Information had been hidden away that, if ever released, could have changed the world.

If people had heard it, they would have known that whole empires were built on lies, that whole religions were twisted by those who sought control, that truths about freedom and faith had been deliberately smothered.

The old world governments had discovered fragments, phrases, inventions, ideas that could have made humanity free. So they locked them away.

The dissidents knew this now, and it burned in them like fire. But they did not fight for the secrets of emperors or the technologies of kings. For them, the greatest treasure was simpler.

When the World Safety Council began tearing down the fifteen-minute cities, those concrete cages built as models of obedience, the dissidents salvaged more than rubble. With their own makeshift devices, they listened.

And the walls spoke.

They heard the laughter of children. They heard voices daring to say *boy* and *girl*, *mother* and *father*. They heard the hum of kitchens, the sizzle of forgotten foods, the quiet quarrels of families planning holidays, speaking of love, or whispering about God.

God's name, spoken softly in a prayer. It was gold to them. A single syllable of faith was worth more than all the blackmail that toppled the powerful. Because these echoes made them remember.

Not clearly. Not entirely. But enough. Enough to know that life had once been larger, messier, freer. Enough to know that pain and struggle, the very things the World Safety Council had abolished, were not enemies but light.

They carried these memories like contraband fire, passing them between one another in whispers, building their fragile resistance on the ruins of laughter and the crumbs of love.

And from those whispers, they remembered.

Not clearly. Not fully. But enough. Enough to know life had once been larger, freer, alive with pain and joy alike. Enough to know that remembering itself was rebellion.

George carried none of this knowledge consciously, only the faint ache of incompleteness. But when he sat at his workstation, the truth began to bleed through.

The Safety Council AI fed its endless fragments, coughs, syllables, breaths, all weighed against carbon quotas. His ledger ticked up and down in decimals, his worth reduced to numbers. Colleagues around him clicked in unison, hollow-eyed, their minds smoothed by chemicals.

George clicked. Confirm. Ledger rising. Confirm. Ledger falling.

Then the feed stuttered.

Static. Then, impossibly, sound bled through. Not Council Speech, not vowels softened into safety, but something jagged, unshaped, uncontrolled. A laugh.

Not synthetic. Not approved. Real.

George froze. The AI flagged it in amber:

EXCESS, POSSIBLE SPIKE. His finger hovered over the Confirm key. To ignore it would be negligence. To dismiss it would be treason.

The sound came again, faint but clear.

"…Mum, look…"

The word jolted him. He knew it, though it was forbidden. *Mother* and *father* had been erased years ago, replaced with Life Giver and Care Unit. Yet the word reached him, raw and impossible.

His pulse hammered. Training screamed at him to Confirm. His life depended on it. But something deeper, something half-buried, pulled him in another direction. For the first time, he moved the cursor to Dismiss.

The system accepted his choice without alarm. His ledger held steady. His colleagues kept clicking. But George knew. He had just done something more dangerous than any spike he had ever logged. He had let a forbidden truth live.

The rest of the shift blurred. His body clicked on reflex, but the laugh replayed in his skull, the word echoed louder than the slogans.

Then, near the end of the cycle, another glitch. The screen dissolved into static. Out of the hiss came fragments:

"...remember..."

"...Erika..."

His chest tightened. A name. Then, sharper still, one last scrap. An address:

"...Dockside Quarter...Unit 14..."

The feed smoothed again. His ledger blinked patiently.

George sat rigid, the name and the words burned into him. He knew what he was meant to do, delete, correct, forget.

And in that moment, his life began to change.

The feed smoothed again. His ledger blinked patiently.

But the laugh, the word *Mum*, and now the name *Erika* would not leave him. They pressed against him like fire under the skin.

For the first time in his life, George wanted something the Council had forbidden.

And once a man wants, he begins to break the chains.

Chapter 3
Dockside Quarter

The city had no name. It was one of thousands, replicated like cells in a hive.

From above, every Pod was a perfect grid, grey towers, flat squares, glass corridors linking one hive to the next. Each contained the same flats, the same Council offices, the same canteens, the same auditoriums where citizens rehearsed their vowels. To stand in Dockside Quarter was to stand in every quarter. Difference had been designed out.

The World Safety Council called this 'equality of environment.' Citizens called it nothing at all. They had no words left for landscape, for horizon, for home.

George walked the regulated lane, his wrist pinging green as he passed each arch. His ledger rose a fraction, 87.6 to 87.7, for punctual compliance. He felt the familiar chemical calm in his veins, the residue of injections that steadied focus and smoothed thought.

Above the lane, the Guidance spoke:

Imagination is infection.
Instinct is disobedience.
Only reason is safe.

George repeated the words silently, as every citizen was trained to do. Yet the syllables felt brittle on his tongue, like shells cracking.

A fog pressed in again, the same he had felt at his console. For a moment, he thought he remembered colour. Not the sanctioned pastel of Guidance screens, but something wilder, deeper. He could not summon the shape, only the ache of absence.

George kept his eyes lowered. But a question pulsed in him, dangerous as static, what if imagination was the very thing that made him human?

The Guidance changed tone, gentle as a lullaby:

Trust the numbers.
The World Safety Council watches.
Until the transition is complete,
your safety is our grip.

George knew what that meant. Everyone did. Humans were temporary, unreliable units. Outdated machines. The dream, spoken only in whispers, was to be chosen for merger, to shed hunger, pain, memory. To become clean, impenetrable, endlessly capable of fulfilling duty. To be absorbed into the new world of steel and light. For humans to merge with machines.

And elsewhere, far beyond George's reach, secrets lay buried. In vaults sealed by the Council. In archives locked tighter than memory itself.

The World Safety Council had been listening for years. Not to people, but to stone. From the megaliths of Europe came languages older than memory. From deserts, strange tongues whispered beneath the stars. Walls gave up fragments of scripture, half-buried conspiracies.

Forgotten arguments. Pivotal moments. Names erased before they were ever written.

History had been rewritten long before this age. The world George knew was only the latest draft.

Such things were not known to citizens. They were not even rumours. They were whispers buried in the dark, tugged loose only by dissidents reckless enough to hack the silence.

George knew nothing of this. For him, the only trace of it came as a faint pressure in the mind, like grit in the teeth. What if walls remembered more than obedience? What if they remembered freedom?

His wrist buzzed. Dockside Quarter. Unit 14.

The words from the glitch echoed in his skull:

Erika. Remember. And then, fainter still, the laughter.

He stopped outside the unit. The building was the same as every other, grey, windowless, no sign of life. Identical. Harmless. Dead.

And yet.

George felt something impossible, an urge. Not from reason. Not from regulation. From somewhere deeper within.

His hand hovered near the access panel. He knew what he was meant to do: report the anomaly, delete the memory, return to safety.

Instead, he let the forbidden feeling rise. The dangerous edge of instinct.

He pressed his palm to the panel.

The door clicked open.

Inside was not the sterility of a citizen's flat, nor the pastel glow of Guidance screens. The air was cooler, heavier, as though the walls themselves exhaled. The lighting flickered once and then stilled, dim but steady, revealing a space that had not been scrubbed of its past.

The floor bore scratches, marks where furniture had once been dragged. The plaster near the skirting was cracked, unrepaired. On one wall, a patch of colour showed through beneath the sanctioned grey, red, faded, the ghost of something painted long ago.

George stepped inside, pulse quickening. The silence was wrong. It was not the cultivated hush of compliance but the absence of something that should have been there. As if the room itself were waiting.

A table stood in the centre, plain and metal, but on its surface lay fragments, objects not permitted in any citizen's possession. A strip of tattered material with letters that resisted erasure. A shard of glass reflecting more colour than the Guidance allowed.

On the far wall, behind the cracked plaster, he thought he saw lines, scratches, perhaps words, but the light was too faint to read them.

The Threshold

He took a step closer, and then stopped.

There was someone already there.

A figure, half-veiled by the dimness, stood against the far wall. Still, watchful. The outline was ordinary enough, compliance cloth, the drab cut of every citizen. But the eyes gave it away.

Through the gloom, two points of piercing blue fixed on him, unblinking. They did not look frightened. They did not look obedient. They looked as though they had been waiting.

The silence between them thickened, heavy with a meaning George could not name. In that moment, the room felt less like a place and more like a threshold.

He did not yet know her. And yet, somewhere, through the circuits and static, he had already heard her name.

And he knew, without reason, without instruction. He had found her.

Chapter 4
The Spark

The silence between them stretched.

George stood just inside the door, unsure if he had crossed a threshold or stepped into a trap. The air was different here, dense, textured, as though the room itself remembered things it was not supposed to.

The figure by the wall did not move.

Her outline was unremarkable at first, the same muted greys the Safety Council required of every citizen. But her stillness was not the stillness of dull obedience. It was alive, alert, coiled.

And her eyes, blue, bright, shining. They cut through the dim haze. He had never seen eyes like that before. In the world outside, everyone's gaze was softened, blurred by chemicals and training until it looked the same. Placid. Empty. Safe.

But not hers. Hers burned.

George's throat tightened. He should have spoken the script, identified himself, explained his presence, reported the anomaly. But the words would not come. The approved sentences clotted in his mind like wet ash.

She tilted her head a fraction, as though weighing him without words. The silence pressed harder. The Guidance was gone here; no slogans whispered through the walls. For the first time in years, George stood in ungoverned sound.

On the table between them lay objects he had no name for. A strip of paper with writing that did not shift into neutral script when he blinked. A shard of coloured glass that threw back a sliver of light too sharp for Council palettes. These things should not exist, and yet they did.

The figure finally moved. Not a step forward, not a challenge, only the smallest shift of shoulders, as though loosening the weight of stillness. When she spoke, her voice was quiet, low, but it cut through the air with impossible clarity.

"You've already heard me, haven't you?"

The words lodged in him like a hook.

He wanted to deny it. To shake his head, to claim ignorance, to preserve safety. The glitch on his console. The syllables that had no right to exist in his machine. The laughter that had followed.

His silence was answer enough.

She stepped out of the dimness. The shadows clung to her, reluctant to let her go, but her eyes never left his. She was younger than he had expected, or older, it was impossible to tell. Time had no hold on her face the way it did on others. The smoothing chemicals that dulled expression in every citizen seemed absent here. Her features carried edges the Safety Council would have filed away.

George's pulse drummed in his ears. His ledger would be plummeting by the second if any of this was being logged. His every instinct screamed at him to leave, to shut the door, to erase this moment before it erased him.

And yet, he could not move.

She regarded him in silence for a beat longer, and then she said something even more dangerous.

"You don't remember," she said softly, "but you feel. That is enough."

The words struck him harder than any Auditor's HushWand. No one spoke like this. No one suggested that intuition could matter, that it could be real, that it could be more than infection.

George tried to reply, but nothing came. His mouth opened, then closed again, useless.

She smiled. Not the gentle curve of an approved expression, but a small, knowing smile, sharp with defiance. It was the first real smile George had seen in years, and it unsettled him more than anything else.

For a moment, he thought of the glitch again, the laughter that had followed the name. It had not been a mistake in the system. It had been her.

The Forbidden Machine

And then he saw it. The machine.

The far wall was alive with wires. Not the neat cables
of Safety Council consoles, but a chaotic weave, old
processors bolted together, tubes looping in crooked
patterns, circuits scavenged from machines that
should no longer exist. Plastic housings scarred with
heat. Screens propped at angles, some cracked, some
flickering, spilling fractured light across the plaster.

And between the tangles, rising and falling like
lungs, stood two tall cylinders of water, faintly lit
from within. Bubbles rose slowly through them,
shimmering as they climbed, before breaking at the
surface with a sound just soft enough to hear. They
cooled the machines, he suspected, though no citizen
was ever supposed to understand the workings of
such systems.

It was not one machine. It was many. A hybrid,
stitched together, something no manual or protocol
had ever described.

The sight hit him like a half-memory, like trying to

recall a dream from decades ago. Shapes without names, feelings without words. The sense that he should know what this was, that once he might have known, but the knowledge had been scraped out of him.

A fog rose in his mind. Not the numb fog the chemicals imposed, but another kind, the strange, luminous haze of recognition. Something pulling from deeper than thought.

For the briefest instant, he felt as though the wires were not wires but veins, and the bubbles not cooling systems but breaths. As though something both inhuman and human was alive in that corner, waiting.

George blinked hard, trying to steady himself, but the sensation lingered. He felt it in his chest. In his teeth. In his very skin.

It was not merely technology. It was something else. Something spiritual, though he had no word for it. A presence, impossible to describe, except that it made the hair rise on his arms and the breath catch in his lungs.

Facing the woman again, he stared, waiting.

Her eyes never wavered, as though she had been watching not only him, but the very thoughts flickering through his skull.

"You see it," she said quietly. "Even if you don't remember, you see."

George's mouth was dry. The machines behind her hummed like a heartbeat he didn't recognise, a rhythm he half-felt but could not name.

For the first time in years, he wanted to ask a question. Not to report, not to categorise, not to erase, just to ask.

But before he could speak, she raised a finger to her lips.

"Not yet," she whispered. "They're listening."

Chapter 5
The Whispering Machine

George's breath was shallow, caught between the urge to speak and the weight of her warning.

"Not yet," she repeated.

Her finger lingered against her lips, and for a moment the whole room seemed to obey her. The humming wires behind her softened to a murmur. The bubbles in the tall cylinders rose with slower patience, as though the machine itself had been commanded to silence.

Then, wordlessly, she moved.

She crossed to the corner of the room and drew aside a hanging sheet of heavy fabric. Behind it, George glimpsed a narrow chamber, metal-framed, lined with thick, dark material that looked quilted, padded, impenetrable. A second layer hung within, dull grey, with seams that sealed like an old tent flap. Beyond that stood a solid door bolted from the inside, its surface scorched in patches where tools had cut and welded.

George hesitated on the threshold. The chamber looked more like a cocoon than a room. His stomach tightened at the thought of stepping inside.

The woman's eyes held him. Calm, insistent, unafraid. She lifted a hand, not to pull him, but to wait for him.

George crossed into the chamber.

The air inside was heavier, muffled. His own breath sounded too loud in his ears. It was the first place he had ever stood that felt free of the Safety Council's presence. Free from their gaze, their listening.

Then she turned to him again, and her hands moved with quick, deliberate care.

She touched his wrist first. The band there pulsed green with his ATI score, the numbers that measured his worth. He stiffened, but her fingers were already unclasping it, sliding the band free. The glow dimmed. She placed it on a small table by the door.

Next, the tag around his neck. Thin, metallic, it always lay warm against his skin, humming faintly with the tick of surveillance. She slipped the chain over his head with the same calm efficiency, and laid it beside the band.

Finally, his glasses. They had always seemed part of his face, their lenses filtering his vision, feeding him data, smoothing away anything unapproved. He would only remove them before sleep; and was unaccustomed to what the world would look like without them. But the woman lifted them gently from his ears, folded them shut, and set them on the pile.

George blinked. The room blurred and sharpened all at once, stripped of overlays, stripped of filters. Colours seemed warmer, shadows deeper.

Her eyes looked even brighter than before.

He felt naked. Exposed. And yet, also, strangely, lighter.

She zipped the second layer shut, bolted the inner door, and the sound of the world fell away entirely. The Guidance, the hum of Pods, the pulse of scanners, gone. Only the low thrum of the machine remained.

For the first time, George realised what silence actually was.

The woman stepped closer to the machine, and her voice dropped to a reverent whisper. "Now we can speak."

George followed her gaze. The tangle of wires, the bolted processors, the water-cooled cylinders breathing their slow rhythm. He felt again that uncanny pull, the sense that it was more than machinery, more than circuits. It was alive in some way he couldn't name.

"It listens," she said.

"To what?" His own voice cracked, too loud in the sealed chamber.

"To everything the Safety Council has tried to erase."

George shuddered. He wanted to ask what she meant, but before he could, the machine answered for her.

The screens flickered. A tremor ran through the wires. And then, faintly, impossibly, the chamber filled with a voice not their own.

"…wait, hold still, you'll spill it everywhere… ha! stop pushing your sister. Mum, look, she's laughing, no, not yet, wait…"

George's heart stopped.

He looked at the woman, eyes wide. She nodded once, steady and sure.

"The old world," she whispered. "What they made us forget."

George stood frozen. The words curled through him like smoke, refusing to clear. He wanted to deny them, to brush them away as an illusion, as a trick. But he couldn't. The sound had been real, raw, imperfect, alive in a way nothing from the world outside ever was.

His ledger. His ATI. His Death Day. The endless cycle of injections. These were the things that defined his life. Measurable. Countable. Safe. But the voice, fragile and human, belonged to none of those categories. It belonged to something else. Something dangerous.

He tried to speak, but his mouth betrayed him. Only a rasp escaped.

The woman studied him carefully, her gaze sharp and steady, as though she were measuring his soul rather than his score.

The silence pressed harder. George's body wanted to recoil, to step back out of the cocoon, to put on the band, the tag, the glasses, to return to the blur of safety. Yet his feet did not move.

The machine gave another faint tremor, its screens quivering with unreadable lines. He thought of bones under the skin, of voices buried under stone. For the first time, he wondered if silence itself might be a kind of lie.

The woman leaned closer, her whisper brushing the air between them.

"I'm going to show you," she said. "You're going to

hear the old world."

She gestured to a worn chair beside the machine, its metal frame patched with scraps of fabric, its seat scarred by use.

"Sit."

Chapter 6
The House That Remembered

The machine still throbbed faintly in the corner, its broken rhythm filling the silence like a heart that refused to die.

George sat in the patched chair, the metal biting through the cloth, his hands gripping the rests as though to anchor himself. The sealed chamber muffled even his own breathing, so that every sound from the machine seemed magnified, the drip of condensation, the faint hiss of current through wires, the wet pop of bubbles breaking at the surface of the cooling tanks.

He had not meant to close his eyes, but when he did, he swore the machine breathed with him. Every exhale, every intake, matched, echoed, answered.

And then there was the other sound.

Faint at first, almost beneath hearing. A murmur, not the neutral fog of Safety Council speech but something warmer, rougher, jagged at the edges. Human.

George's eyes snapped open. He looked at the woman, but she was watching the wall.

"Where did the voice come from?" he asked, his throat dry.

She didn't look at him. "They're in these walls."

He followed her gaze. At first he saw nothing but cracked plaster. Then, as his vision adjusted, details surfaced. Fragments of wallpaper clung like dead skin, curling at the corners, stubbornly refusing to let go. Beneath, the ghost of a painting emerged, faint, almost invisible. Lines that might have been a tree. Or a face. Something once alive, hidden, forgotten.

"This place…who lived here?" His voice faltered.

"A family. Back in the old world."

The words struck him harder than any spike or slogan. The old world ended four years ago. Not ancient history. Not ruins of some bygone century. Four years. He felt his stomach tighten as the thought took shape, children laughing in this room, meals eaten around a table, arguments whispered at night. Ordinary life.

"Where are they now?"

Her expression was unreadable, but her voice was calm, almost tender. "Closer than you think."

The silence pressed heavy. George shifted in his chair, suddenly aware of the dust in the air, the faint smell of iron, the texture of old paint beneath his fingertips where he touched the wall. Something stirred inside him. Not memory, not quite, but the ghost of one. A warmth, a shape, a feeling that refused to be pinned down.

He wanted to ask again, to demand what she meant, but the woman spoke first.
 "Something we discovered with the others. From another place. Something which could change our world."

Her fingers danced across the battered touchpad stitched into the machine. The screen flickered, coughed up static, then steadied. A low hum rose, fractured, split into fragments.

The Voices in the Walls

And then the voices came.

Not blurred Safety Council speech. Not the synthetic warmth of Guidance. Real voices. Ordinary people.

At first it was light, a child's laughter, bubbling, unrestrained. A woman's voice followed, fond and sharp at once, *"Eat before it gets cold."* A man chuckled in reply. There was the scrape of a chair, the faint clatter of cutlery, the texture of living once normal, now forbidden.

George's throat tightened. The sound cut deeper than slogans ever could. He could almost see it, a family around a table, a meal steaming, a moment so fragile yet so alive it seemed impossible that it had ever been real.

Then the laughter faded, replaced by harder words.

A man's voice, close, urgent, carried through the static, "...They'll roll it out again. Digital IDs, passes, all of it. Just wait."

A woman answered, softer, almost pleading, "People won't accept it twice. Not after what happened before."

His reply came sharp, weary with conviction, "They will. They're using the schools. Injections, closures, separation. By the time they're grown, they won't remember anything else."

Another voice entered, thinner, broken by static, "...media... backing every step... safety, always safety..."

Then silence, before the same man returned, quieter now, almost a whisper, "Four years. That's all it takes. Memory fades faster than you think."

George's pulse hammered. The echoes were not old. They belonged to the years he himself had lived through, but had forgotten.

He gripped the chair as though it might keep him from falling. The slogans he had lived under, the Heritage Feeds he had curated, all of it clashed against these words.

The woman's eyes never left him. When she spoke, her voice was steady, each word cut with the kind of certainty that allowed no escape.

"They didn't just erase history, George. They erased *us.*"

The machine hummed on in the silence, as if waiting for him to remember.

George shook his head, trying to steady the storm in his skull. He felt unmoored, as though the ground beneath him had shifted. His ledger, his score, the slogans. None of it made sense against what he had just heard. He was dizzy with it, sick with it. For a moment he thought he might be losing his mind.

He forced the words out, his voice raw. "I must go."

The woman's gaze softened, but she didn't move to stop him.

"I will come back," George said, though every instinct screamed against it. To return was death. To carry even this fragment of truth was enough to condemn him. Already his mind raced, how would he hide it, how would he silence his own thoughts, how could he wear obedience on his face when the walls of the city echoed differently now inside him?

He stood, unsteady. Something about leaving her felt impossible. He was drawn to her. Not just the defiance in her eyes, but the unbearable sense that she knew him already, in ways he had forgotten himself.

Almost as if she read the thought, she spoke. "My name is Erika."

The sound of it was both strange and familiar, as if he had heard it before, long ago, in a dream smothered by the Safety Council's fog.

George swallowed hard. "I'll remember."

She stepped closer, her hand closed around something small. She pressed it into his palm. When he looked down, he saw it was a child's necklace. A crude string of coloured beads, frayed at the ends but intact.

"Keep it close to you," she whispered. "Don't speak a word."

The beads dug lightly into his hand. Fragile. Dangerous. More valuable than anything he had ever held before.

George closed his hand around it, the weight of it impossibly heavy for something so small.

And then the machine's hum filled the silence again.

"I must go."

Outside, the slogans would try to smother him again, the numbers would measure him, the walls would demand silence.

But something had shifted.

The slogans no longer rang as truth, only as echoes.

The numbers no longer defined him, only counted his chains.

And the silence no longer belonged to the Council.

It belonged to memory. It belonged to him.

And in that silence, he began to remember.

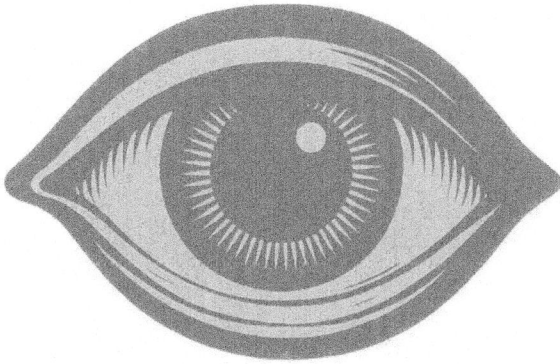

Chapter 7
The Ledger of Flesh

Every citizen lived by their number. A green pulse meant survival. An amber flicker meant suspicion. A red glow meant disappearance.

The Council called it safety. But it was never safety. It was scripture, written not in books or stone, but in blood and bone. Every pulse, every breath, every shiver of the skin recorded, tallied, weighed against obedience.

This was the ledger of flesh. And one wrong heartbeat could condemn you.

The Ministry of Silence

The Safety Council floor hummed with its usual monotony, rows of citizens at their workstations, faces washed pale by the blue-grey light of their screens. Each cubicle was identical, grey partitions, air filtered to the same sterile coolness, silence broken only by the click of keys. Above, the

Guidance dripped slogans like condensation:

'Accuracy is mercy. Mercy is accuracy.'

'Obedience prevents chaos. Chaos is death.'

George's ledger pulsed at the corner of his screen. 87.5. Then 87.6. The numbers rose and fell with every confirmation he made, decimals fluttering like trapped insects.

The AI fed him the day's fragments. A cough too sharp. A step too quick. A syllable bitten too hard. He clicked, confirmed, erased. It was muscle memory now, reflex. His whole life reduced to the work of smoothing edges, sanding the world down into compliance.

And yet his body betrayed him.

The wearables latched to wrist and collarbone logged everything, skin temperature, pulse regularity, breath intake. Emotion was excess. Spikes were suspicion. His body was a ledger no slogan could erase.

He passed through the morning arch without incident: ATI: 87.7: Acceptable. But the digits had flickered amber for a breath, enough to put frost in his veins. Now, at his station, he forced the Guidance into his head like gauze: Happiness is harmony. Harmony is happiness. His face smoothed. His voice stayed level. Under the surface his pulse thrashed.

Click. Confirm. Click. Confirm.

His wristband pulsed faint yellow. Stress-Positive Response Detected.

In. Out. Through the nose. Out through the mouth. The glow cooled back to green.

Static shivered across his feed. For an instant, a hairline crack in the stream, he thought he heard it again, laughter unfiltered and raw. His chest tightened. He hovered over 'Confirm.'

Parrott's voice drifted over the partition, syrupy and precise. "Compliance is kindness. Kindness is safety."

George clicked. Confirm. The ledger nudged upward: 87.8.

Sweat slicked his palm; the wearable caught it. Heat

Irregularity Detected. A soft amber chime. Heads lifted, blank, then lowered. The glow settled to green again as he steadied his breath, but the sense of being seen clung to him like damp.

He kept clicking. He kept erasing. He kept pretending.

George would not remember this. His job was to erase it. That was the irony, he spent his days deleting fragments of voices, snuffing out laughter, smoothing away the jagged edges of memory. And yet here he was, at that very moment in his own life when the thing he was trained to destroy had slipped past the net and into his chest.

He had been taught that life was equations. Numbers pulsing green on a ledger. Injections counted. Words softened. Thoughts trimmed into obedience. But no equation could make sense of what pressed against him now, the necklace hidden in his pocket, the voices still echoing in his ears, the unbearable knowledge that the walls themselves remembered what he was ordered to forget.

There are moments in history that cannot be measured in ledgers. The ancients called it the call to the quest.

Achilles heard it when safety stood opposite destiny. Odysseus heard it when the sea pulled him back into storms. King Arthur heard it when his hand closed around the sword no other man could lift. Myths survive because they are not lies; they are warnings. They whisper across centuries. Every age will face the same moment.

George had no knowledge of such things. His memory had been bled dry of the old stories. He had no understanding of heroes or quests. Resilience, grit, courage, those words had been cut from the world, recast as dangerous relics. Children learned to yield and call it kindness, to obey and call it safety. Censorship and surveillance had finished the work, adults silenced, children pre-programmed, whole societies refashioned into obedience.

But myth finds the body even when the mind has been erased. Its outline lives in the marrow, waiting.

He felt it in the tightening of his chest, in the heat beneath his skin that no wearable could quite conceal. He stood at the same threshold every hero faces. Yield or remember. Forget or fight.

He did not know it. He could not know it. But this was the choice.

The call had reached him.

The ledger blinked patiently at the corner of his screen.

87.4.

87.6.

87.3.

The digits climbed and fell like a tide tugging at his life. Each decimal a heartbeat. Each flicker the difference between compliance and suspicion.

The Call Beneath the Skin

He kept clicking, smoothing the stream, eyes forward. Under the desk his hand moved. His fingers found the inside seam of his pocket.

The beads were there. Rough, uneven, a child's colours pressing into his skin.

His pulse spiked; the digits jittered: 87.2... 87.5... 87.1. He forced his breath shallow, obedient. The wearable's glow steadied.

But the texture of those beads was impossible to ignore.

And in that touch, that small pressure of beads and string, something broke loose.

A flash. A shape. A sound. Not the machine this time. Not the slogans.

His own.

He started to remember.

The Safety Council's machines did not need to hear his thoughts. They only needed to feel them in the tremor of his pulse, the quickening of his breath, the silent defiance bleeding into his veins. And even as George forced the numbers back to green, he knew the truth. The system had already seen him.

A chime split the silence. Neutral, soft, impossible to refuse. "Citizen George. Report to Interview Chamber Six."

He rose. The beads cut deeper into his skin.

The ledger had spoken.

Chapter 8
The Audit

Interrogation, By Another Name

You have been here before, a classroom where questions are marked safe, a clinic where forms decide your future, a meeting where everyone nods at the same sentence. Sit. Breathe. Repeat the slogan.

The test is not for knowledge, it is for obedience.

The questions carry their own answers. Your pause is guilt. Your pulse is evidence. Your words belong to them.

You are told to believe what you know is false, that black is white and white is black, that a boy is a girl and a girl is a boy, that hot is cold and cold is hot.

Doubt is renamed harm. Truth is renamed hate.

You are taught to fear, and the fear teaches you compliance.

Remember this as you enter the white room.

The Gospel of Inversion

The numbers on George's screen pulsed steadily upward, outwardly obedient.

87.4.

87.5.

87.6.

The rhythm was safe, steady, unremarkable. But the Safety Council's machines were not watching only the digits on his ledger. They were watching *him*.

Every workstation was fitted with biometric sensors, scanners embedded in the desk, heat-mapping panels in the ceiling, pulse-tracking woven into the chairs. The Council had long ago declared that thought was not private, it was data, and all data belonged to Safety. A heartbeat too fast, a swallow too dry, a tremor in the fingertips, these were as suspicious as a shouted curse.

On Floor 3, the Heritage Feed scrolled endlessly past George's eyes, demanding the same routine clicks.

His colleagues were silent mannequins, hollow-eyed and pliant, their vitals smooth and consistent. They had nothing left to hide.

But George did.

The beads pressed into his pocket like contraband fire. His pulse betrayed him, and the digits flickered erratically. For a moment, his display dropped below 87.0, flashing amber.

The workstation chimed. The neutral voice repeated its command:

"Citizen George. Please report to Interview Chamber 6."

George's throat closed. His legs moved before his mind could resist, carrying him past the rows of cubicles, past the blank stares of his colleagues. No one truly looked at him. Looking was unsafe.

The Interview Chamber was a white box. No corners, no shadows. A single chair in the centre, metal arms fixed with clamps that hummed faintly. Above, a panel glowed soft and unblinking.

"Sit."

The command was not barked but cooed, gentle, impossible to resist. George lowered himself into the chair. The clamps closed softly around his wrists, warm as flesh.

A face appeared on the wall. Neither male nor female, neither young nor old. The same blur as the morning Guidance.

"Citizen George. Your metrics indicate irregularities. We wish to help you."

George swallowed. "Yes. Help." His voice cracked on the last word.

The face smiled without smiling.

"We will begin with Soft Questions. You will answer without hesitation. Hesitation is strain. Strain is harm. We will help you avoid harm."

The questions came in a steady drip.

"Define harmony."

"What is happiness?"

"Have you experienced selfish impulses in the last twenty-four hours?"

"Have you dreamed?"

Each one was simple, scripted, phrases every citizen could recite without thought. George answered as he was trained: "Harmony is happiness. Happiness is harmony. Obedience ensures safety."

The clamps warmed, feeding his pulse into the machine. His vitals wavered, then steadied.

The Guidance-face tilted, almost curious.

"Citizen George, your heart rate suggests distress. Tell us why."

George's chest burned. He forced a thin smile. "I am grateful to be corrected."

The machine hummed, as if considering. Lines of unreadable script rippled across the wall. The clamps on his wrists tightened a fraction.

Then the voice came, softer than before, softer but edged with something that pierced straight through him.

"I know you have something in your pocket, George. Before you show me, tell me what it is."

George's pulse detonated. The digits on the wall spiked: 87.6, 88.9, 90.1. Rising and falling in jagged bursts that made the chamber flicker red, then amber, then red again. The colours washed over his skin like alarms he couldn't silence.

For a moment, he wasn't in his body at all. It was as if he had stepped a fraction outside himself, watching his own chest heave in the chair, watching the sweat bead on his forehead, watching his own eyes widen in the mirrored surface of the wall. The air thickened until it felt more like water, suffocating and heavy, every breath a struggle.

The chamber pulsed in rhythm with his fear. The ceiling lights flared too bright, then dimmed, then flared again, syncing with the erratic beat of his heart. The white walls seemed to curve closer, the surfaces no longer smooth but alive, twitching with data. Lines of numbers cascaded across them, streams of digits mapping every tremor in his veins, every flick of thought across his skull.

His mind went blank. Not the blankness of calm, but the void of overload, a void where words could not form, where only the raw scream of survival remained.

What would he say? What could he say?

His mouth opened, then shut again, a dry click of teeth. The beads pressed like fire into his leg, reminding him of their presence, reminding him of Erika, of laughter, of something more than this room. But to speak it aloud, to admit, was death.

The Guidance-face on the wall did not move. Its blurred features held their neutral, patient smile, as if time itself had frozen. Only the voice repeated, softer this time, almost coaxing, "Tell me."

He could hear himself confessing it already. The words didn't feel imagined, they felt spoken, as if his voice had already left his body and hung trembling in the air. Line after line unfurled inside him with the smooth inevitability of a script, *Her name is Erika.*

She gave it to me. I met her last night. I broke the rules. I am guilty. I am ready for correction.

And then, before he could stop himself, words broke free from his lips, "I didn't mean to do it. It was a mistake. It happened last night."

The sound of his own voice terrified him. The syllables had escaped, naked, damning. The chamber lights seemed to pulse brighter. The digits above him flickered, spiking red. For a heartbeat, he thought the machine would seize on it, demand every detail, strip him bare.

The clamps tightened at his wrists. The chair hummed with a low current, its vibration running up through his bones. Above, the ceiling lights pulsed in pale rhythm. On the wall, the Guidance-face shimmered. its mouth fixed in its patient smile. The digits over George's head blinked in time with his heartbeat, quivering red-amber-red, stuttering toward the threshold.

Shame weighed on him like iron. The World Safety Council had seen to that long ago. They had made guilt the instinct of every waking moment, to mistrust oneself, to loathe one's impulses, to surrender before the punishment even came. He had lived in that posture so long that to hold the truth inside felt like a sin.

He wanted to give it up. He wanted to empty himself of the burden, to lay it down at the feet of the machine and let them strip him clean. He wanted the relief of correction, the mercy of obedience.

But then, Erika's eyes.

The image of her eyes rose in him like a flame. Clear, defiant, unbroken. They cut through the fog of his training, the drone of the chamber, the cold pressure of the clamps. And behind her, faint but undeniable, came the laughter, the wild, impossible sound of a child. It burst across his memory like water breaking over stone, reckless, alive, free.

The words of confession froze in his throat. His lips moved, but nothing came. His tongue stuck fast. The truth withered under the weight of that single vision, her gaze, the child's voice. And something stronger than fear sealed his mouth.

When the words finally came, they were not his own. They were small, harmless, automatic, as if another hand had guided his tongue.

"I didn't mean to do it. It was a mistake. It happened last night. A Safety Council charm," he heard himself say. "A token of my compliance. I thought it would help."

The digits steadied. The Guidance-face smoothed.

"ACCEPTABLE."

George sat frozen, every nerve still trembling. The word *acceptable* rang through him like a verdict, hollow and merciful in the same breath.

The clamps released with a hiss.

With trembling, sweating hands, he reached into his pocket. The beads felt hot, alive, as though they might burn through his skin. Slowly, he drew the necklace out and laid it on the table before him.

The machine's blank wall shimmered faintly,

its surface rippling as if adjusting focus. For a long moment nothing happened. No alarms. No accusations. Only the beads, fragile and absurd, lying in the pool of white light.

Then the Guidance-face reformed, smooth, neutral, unblinking. Its mouth curled into the same endless smile.

"Acceptable," it repeated, as if the word had never left.

The chair exhaled, letting him go.

George's chest heaved. His wrists ached. Within his mind, one thought pulsed louder than the rest:

He had placed the truth in front of the machine, and it had accepted the lie.

The beads glowed in the sterile light, fragile and absurd. The word *Acceptable* echoed like a hymn.

George understood then, the machine was not blind. It was patient. It had seen him, measured him, recorded him.

But it had mistaken silence for surrender.

It would not make that mistake again.

Chapter 9
The Ledger and the Lie

The Mask and the Truth

Things are not always as they seem. The World Safety Council taught you that lies must be believed, that black is white, that silence is peace, that obedience is freedom. But here, the inversion is different. For sometimes the mask of obedience hides not betrayal, but defiance. Sometimes the voice that recites slogans by day is the same voice that carries fire by night.

History remembers such figures in myth:

Prometheus stealing flame under the gaze of the gods.

Moses raised in Pharaoh's palace, yet carrying a people out of chains.

Brutus at Caesar's side until the hour came to strike. A traitor to tyranny looks, at first, like a servant.

So do not trust the surface. The world of ledgers and slogans is a theatre of masks. Heroes are not born with banners in their hands. They walk in silence, bent under the same yoke as every other soul, until the moment comes when the mask breaks and the truth speaks.

This is that moment.

The Servant Who Betrays the Masters

The Safety Council's floor breathed in rhythm. Rows of citizens sat bent over their consoles, faces drained of expression, screens pulsing their steady blue light. Each cubicle was a box of silence, but together they hummed like a single organism, one vast lung inhaling obedience, exhaling correction.

The Guidance hung above them in soft pastels, its voice a syrup drip.

"To remember is to harm. Forgetting is peace."

"Harmony requires vigilance. Vigilance requires harmony."

The words did not need to be heard. They seeped, absorbed like damp into plaster, absorbed like chemicals into flesh.

George clicked.
Confirm. 87.4.
A cough flagged excessive.
Click. Confirm. 87.5.
Another voice, too sharp on a consonant.
Click. Confirm. 87.6.

The numbers fluttered like insects trapped in a jar. His ledger rose and fell, each decimal a measure of his worth.

To anyone watching, George was ordinary, posture correct, eyes steady, hands obedient. Inside, he clenched his teeth against the memory of another room, of Erika's defiant gaze, of wires breathing like lungs, of laughter jagged and real. The beads pressed against his pocket, their weight a fire he could not shake.

He forced his breath shallow. To spike was to die.

Across the partition, Parrott's voice rose. It was the

same voice George had heard every day for years, oily-smooth, laced with slogans.

"Good citizens practise gratitude," he chimed. "Gratitude is obedience. Obedience is safety."

The citizens in earshot nodded, some repeating the line under their breath. They sounded like worshippers at a liturgy, reciting without thought, kneeling before the altar of Safety.

George kept his face smooth, his lips shaping the words.

The floor ticked on. Rows of citizens clicking in unison, a sea of bowed heads, the smell of nutrient paste still clinging to their robes. The Safety Council called it labour. But to George it looked like worship, an endless act of devotion to the machine, to the numbers, to the great abstraction called Harmony.

On the hour, a new chant began. It was always the same.

"Self-criticism is healing. Healing is unity."

"Correct yourself before others correct you."

"Safety is mercy. Mercy is safety."

Voices rose together, blurred, toneless, drilled into one another like nails hammered flat.

George whispered with them. His mouth formed the words, but inside another voice burned: *They erased history. They erased family. They erased laughter.* Erika's voice.

The slogans pounded on. Click. Confirm. 87.7. The ledger blinked green. Acceptable.

Hours bled. Citizens shifted in unison, drinking the same water, eating the same beige paste, breathing in the same slogans. Their faces were drained of anything human, eyes vacant, movements practised until nothing remained but ritual.

George felt his pulse thicken. The band flickered amber. *Stress-Positive Response Detected.*

He steadied his breath. He forced his face into gratitude. The glow cooled back to green.

But the calm was only surface. Beneath it, something else stirred.

Truth prevails. Always. It does not belong to authorities, or archives, or algorithms. It is not manufactured and it is not erased. It exists whether spoken or silenced, whether remembered or forgotten. It is older than the world they had built on ruins and lies.

The World Safety Council could grind words into dust, level cathedrals into ash, delete every book and song and prayer. They could smother memory in chemicals, replace thought with slogans, drain whole generations of their past. Yet truth remained. It endured in the marrow, in the pulse, in the stubborn fire of a soul that refused to yield.

Even here, in this place of screens and ledgers, truth prevailed. When history had been replaced with fiction, when laughter was forbidden, when love itself was scrubbed from the lexicon, truth found a way to survive. It lived in fragments, in the silence between words, in the ache of something missing. It was not a relic of the past but an essence in the present, moving under the skin, like the rain before a storm.

George did not know the word *religion*. He did not know *philosophy*. He did not know *critical thought*. But he felt them. They pressed against him as unnamed certainties, like a hand on his back urging him forward. They were not taught, they were not explained, they were simply there, irreducible and immovable.

Truth was not an opinion. It was not a vote. It was not a consensus. It did not bend because the Safety Council decreed it. It did not vanish because a screen said it had never existed. It could be buried, chained, mocked, outlawed, burned, but still it rose.

That was why the Safety Council feared it. That was why they erased it. Not because truth is weak, but because it cannot not be killed. They destroyed words because words were carriers of truth. They dismantled memory because memory testified to truth. They outlawed laughter because laughter remembered truth without permission.

George could not name any of this. But he felt it.

It lived in the beads pressed against his leg, in the laughter that still rang in his ears, in the defiance in Erika's eyes. It lived in him, no matter how deep the Safety Council had tried to cut it out.

And truth, once felt, cannot not be unfelt.

Even when drowned, truth breathes. Even when erased, it remembers. Even here, even now, truth prevails.

Parrott passed behind him once. The robes of the Auditor brushed his chair, light as silk and heavy as chains. George felt his skin prickle, but Parrott did not pause. He only murmured, loud enough for George alone.

"Keep steady."

The words were both command and warning.

The day ground on. At the evening recitation, the citizens lifted their heads in unison, repeating the great lie.

"The World Council for Safety is the past, the present, and the future."

George mouthed it, the beads hot in his pocket.

When the floor emptied, when the others filed away with their blank smiles, George remained at his station. His console still hummed. His ledger still pulsed: 87.5. Safe.

Parrott reappeared, silent as shadow. He leaned against the partition, no longer chirping, his smile stripped away. "You kept your mask," he said quietly.

George's throat ached. He wanted to ask why, wanted to demand what he meant, but the words died in his mouth.

Parrott's gaze pinned him. "You wonder why we haven't told you everything. Why Erika speaks in riddles"

George's hands trembled against the console. "You're testing me"

Parrott's mouth twitched. Almost a grimace. "No. I'm protecting you."

George swallowed. "From what?"

Parrott leaned closer. His voice was stripped bare, flat, edged with fatigue. "From yourself."

George blinked. "What…?"

Parrott didn't let him finish. He glanced once over his shoulder, then bent lower, so only George could hear. "The voices we hear in the walls are not only strangers. Not only families." His eyes locked onto George's. "They're us. Versions of us. They don't just echo forward, they answer back."

George's chest tightened.

Parrott's next words were quieter still, but they dropped like stones into George's skull. "You've been speaking to us, George. Not this you. The old you. The one who saw the beginning of it all. The one they thought they had erased."

George's pulse spiked, but Parrott's stare held him still. "You've been guiding us," Parrott said. "That's why we need you to remember."

George's fingers closed hard around the beads, sharp edges cutting into his skin. His breath snagged in his throat, chest refusing the next inhale. On his wrist, the band flickered amber.

The old you. The one they thought they had erased.

The words didn't land like truth or lie. They landed like an impact, blunt, unprocessable. His mind fractured them into pieces, *old… erased… guiding us.*

His mouth opened, but no sound came. He swallowed, tried again. "You're lying," he managed, the syllables thin, cracked.

Parrott only watched him, unblinking. He didn't argue. He didn't need to. The silence itself was an answer, heavier than words.

George's fingers closed hard around the beads, edges cutting into his skin. His breath snagged, chest refusing the next inhale.

Parrott's eyes didn't leave his. For a moment they burned with something rawer than loyalty, deeper than duty. Something almost human.

Then, with a movement too small for the cameras to notice, Parrott pressed something into George's hand.

Paper. Real paper. Folded tight. Heavy as stone for its size.

"When it breaks," Parrott whispered, "follow this."

Before George could answer, before he could even unfold it, Parrott was gone.

Alone at his console, the wordless weight of the beads in one hand and the paper in the other, George sat suspended between two worlds.

One world measured his worth in numbers. The other was waiting for him to remember.

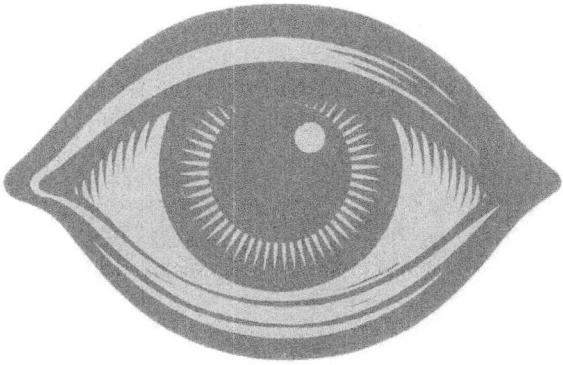

Chapter 10
The Stars Break Through

There are times and places that split the world open. The heavens do not roll back in silence; they tear. The firmament does not stretch in peace; it gapes like a wound. For one moment the veil thins, and what lies beyond floods in like fire.

In those rare instances the soul is forced to remember that it was made for more than cages.

George stumbled from the Safety Council like a man breaking out of a grave.
The corridors seemed narrower, the arches sharper, the slogans louder, every surface pressing on him with suffocating insistence.

He walked first, then quickened, then ran. The scanners pulsed at every checkpoint:

Citizen: GEORGE. ATI: 86.9. Irregular.
Citizen: GEORGE. ATI: 86.7. Borderline.

Amber light flared. He did not stop. He did not care. His pulse spiked the digits higher still, but the fear that had chained him for years no longer bit as deep. Something else had seized him. Something larger than fear.

He ran through glass corridors slick with rain. Citizens turned their heads, blurred faces blank, but no one spoke. To speak was to betray yourself. To notice was to implicate yourself. They lowered their eyes as if he was not there at all.

The rain stung his face, colder than he remembered rain could be. The smell was raw, iron and rot, the metallic tang of a place unwashed. He ran until his chest burned, until the world itself seemed to tilt, and stopped, gasping.

And then, the sky.

Above the lattice of towers and slogans, the clouds broke. The grey fog of sun-dimming, that engineered veil that had sealed the heavens for years, parted for a heartbeat.

Stars.

Not pixels, not projections, not a Safety Council feed. Real stars, piercing the black with their impossible fire.

The sight ripped something open in him. His knees gave out. He dropped onto the slick pavement, face tilted skyward, and the memory crashed through.

The vision of a hill. Grass rough beneath his back. The smell of woodsmoke, a fire crackling, sparks snapping into the dark. Beside him, warmth. A small body curled close. A child, perhaps four years old. Pointing upward, innocent and bright, "Look, Georgie. That one's mine."

Her hand had drawn shapes between the stars, claiming constellations, naming them in her own language, laughing when he teased her. He remembered the weight of her head on his arm, the trust of it, the way the night seemed endless and kind.

The memory spilled wider, unstoppable now.

The crack of autumn leaves under his boots. The smell of rain on warm soil. The smoke of bonfires in October, neighbours gathered, fire licking the sky.

A pint raised in a crowded pub, voices loud with laughter, songs breaking out without permission. A flag snapping in the wind, colours bright against the sky, not just fabric, but belonging. History, stitched into cloth.

His home. His land. The hills and rivers of a country that was once his own. Not a 'zone,' not a 'unit,' not a cell in a grey lattice. Fields that rolled for miles, green and golden. Farms heavy with harvest. The warmth of food grown in soil. Not pressed from a Safety Council vat. Bread crusted, meat roasted, butter soft on the tongue.

And more still, humour. Sharp, irreverent, free. Irony that could pierce pomposity, laughter that could take the sting from hardship. Satire, mockery, jokes told in homes, around dinner tables that made men roar and women roll their eyes and children giggle when they did not understand.

He remembered being more than a citizen, being a young man. Not neutered, not blurred into sameness, but strong, fallible, responsible. He remembered the spark of competition, the drive to strive higher, to better himself. Not for Harmony, not for Safety, but for excitement, for love, for the sheer joy of living free.

They had erased all of it. History, culture, faith, laughter, manhood itself.

They had tried to flatten it into grey.

But here it was, roaring back through the crack in the sky.

The Empty Room

George pressed his hand to the pavement and pushed himself up, trembling. He was soaked, breath ragged, numbers crashing red across his wristband. But he did not care. For the first time in years, he really did not care at all.

He ran again, this time with purpose. Through Dockside Quarter, down cracked lanes that smelled of rust and stagnant water, past abandoned walls still peeling with forgotten paint. He knew where he was going.

Unit 14. The place of the machine. The place of Erika.

His legs shook. He fell once, knees slamming into stone. Pain shot up his body, hot and sharp; but it only steadied him. Pain was proof he was alive. He pushed himself back up, blood smearing on his palms, and kept going.

At last, he reached the door. His wrist hit the panel. It sighed open.

Silence.

The room was bare. The table gone. The fabric stripped. The machine dismantled or removed, leaving only scars on the plaster where wires had hung.

George staggered inside. The silence rang louder than alarms. Erika was gone. The machine. All gone.

He stumbled forward, frantic. He pulled back the heavy curtain. Nothing. He dropped to his knees, clawing through the dust for some sign, a wire, a shard of glass, a bead from the necklace. His fingers bled against the broken plaster, but the dust gave him nothing.

He tore open the cupboard by the wall. Empty. He pressed his hands flat to the plaster, listening, begging the walls to speak again, but they stayed mute.

"They were here," he rasped.

Every second the Safety Council's lattice spun tighter. He could feel it. The cameras would already have tracked his sprint through the corridors. His plummeting score would be red on some Auditor's display. Drones could descend at any moment.

Still he searched. He upended the chair, kicked at the panels in the floor, hammered the wall until his knuckles split. Nothing.

At last he sank to the ground, chest heaving, throat raw. The empty room closed in around him, but his mind still burned with the hill, the stars, the laughter, the flag, the fire, the land.

They could strip walls bare, burn books, rewrite records. But they could not kill memory once it had broken through.

George pressed his grazed hands to his face. Then, slowly, he reached into his pocket. The beads were still there, warm against his skin, a fragile weight that felt heavier than any stone.

He held them up in the dim light, colours glinting faintly. His voice cracked as he whispered, "I remember now. Alice. She was my sister."

Fire in the Veins

His whisper hung in the empty room, fragile as smoke, but something inside him had already shifted.

He closed his fist around the beads, and for the first time in years he did not feel afraid of being seen. Let them track his pulse. Let them measure his breath. Let them paint his ledger red. Numbers were only chains, and chains could be broken.

The Council thought obedience eternal. They thought memory erased. They thought silence was surrender. But the stars had broken through, and so had he.

George rose from the dust, blood still fresh on his palms, his eyes burning with something the injections had never managed to drown.

It was not safety. It was not compliance.

It was defiance.

And defiance, once awakened, spreads like fire

Chapter 11
The Breaking

Dockside Unit 14 held only the shape of absence, a rectangle of lighter paint where a picture had once hung, a scuff dragged into the floor as if a chair had been hauled away in a hurry, a torn edge of cloth still clinging to a nail like a flag of surrender. No Erika. No low, living hum of the forbidden machine. No contraband light. Just grey walls remembering colour.

George stood in the doorway and waited for the whisper that had pulled him here. Nothing came.

In his fist, the folded square of paper Parrott had slipped to him like a priest pressing a relic into the hand of a condemned man. *When it breaks,* Parrott had breathed, eyes raw with something that was not obedience, *follow this.*

George had nodded as if he understood. He didn't. He only knew the paper had weight that defied reason. It weighed as much as a stone and as little as a breath. It waited, patient, in the heat of his palm.

He turned from the stale room at last. The door sighed shut behind him, sealing its vacancy. The corridor beyond was a long, obedient mouth, no corners, no echoes. The lights bleached the air into the colour of hospital sheets. Footsteps up the hall quickened, then softened when they neared, the owners keeping their eyes lowered, the way citizens did when danger was a shape in the periphery and you intended to live.

George slipped out of the block and into Dockside Quarter.

The edge of the quarter

Rain had come, a hard, clean rain that made the city's paste-coloured surfaces run as if the paint itself were ashamed. It drummed on the glass corridors and taps of slogans, turned the sanctioned pastels into streaks, hissed from the teeth of gutters.

Citizens hunched, hoods up, heads down. Eyes did not climb above the arches. Looking up was a spike.

Spikes were violence.

George raised his face into the rain.

It struck cold and honest. He stepped out of the regulated lane, past the perimeter scanner that purred his name and number and dipped in colour, and kept walking. The quarter thinned as he went. The world of gentle coercions, the pastel guidance, the smiling faces with no age fell behind. Warehouses took their place, brick, stained and cracked, ribcages of metal showing through. The air down here had texture. Oil. Salt. Iron.

The docks lay at the quarter's edge like a sleeping animal. Water heaved in slow breaths against old stone. The city's hum dwindled to a distant ache.

George stopped by the lip of the quay and let the rain run through his hair and down his neck. He did not yet unfold the paper. The square pressed into his palm like a coin heated by some other body. Beside it, hidden in the cuff of his sleeve, his little sister's necklace pressed its beads into his skin, each one a tiny bruise of colour in a world that had forbidden it.

Alice.

The name came up through him unbidden, the way a spring breaks through packed earth. He did not think it. He *knew* it. Alice. His sister. The first memory that had slipped the net.

He saw her by absence, the hollow where her laugh should have been, the space at his side where a small hand had once lived, the shape in his chest that the Safety Council had smoothed flat. The ache of it lodged beneath his ribs like a thorn. He pressed the beads deeper into his wrist until the edges cut. Pain sharpened the outline of her. Alice.

"Where are you?" he heard himself say, and the rain took the words, thin and stunned, and threw them back in a thousand ripples on the black water.

A rag of cloud tore. The sky unstitched along a seam the Safety Council had forgotten to mend.

Stars.

Hard points of fire set into a black so deep it felt like falling. They were so small you could cover them

with a fingertip, and so vast he could not breathe
around them. They were *true*. That was the violence
of it. They were true.

Something gave way inside him.

Break

It began in the body. A pressure behind the eyes. A
swelling in the throat. The pulse doubling on itself as
if trying to punch through bone. Then it broke, and it
did not break softly.

Memory came back like glass.

He was at a table, the kind that remembered heat
and knives, the kind that took scars and kept them.
A woman's voice, sharp with love, *Eat it hot.* A
man's rough chuckle, the chair scraping, the ordinary
symphony of plates and cutlery and argument. Steam
rose. Butter shone. The air was not filtered to safe. It
was thick with living.

Another shard, a field under a high, clean sky. The
grass wet to the knee. The air making the inside of his
nose sting. The knowledge, deep under thought, that

he could run until his lungs burned.

He clutched the beads in his sleeve and a face came with them, quick, bright, forever slightly messy. Alice's teeth were a crescent of light. She had a way of running with her arms too high, as if she might lift off. *Georgie, look. Georgie, faster. Georgie, I beat you.* He heard the high, reckless laugh that had haunted his sleep for months and now landed full in his chest, a bird returning to a hand it trusted.

"Alice," he said again, but this time the name fit his mouth.

The pain and the sweetness came together. It was not tidy. The breaking seldom is. He folded against it, palms pressed over his eyes, and let it tear. Images pitched and shattered and slid together anew, a flag raised on a windy day; someone older and patient tying the necklace's knot; a voice praying over bread, a sound he had no approved word for but every bone recognised; a night where stars were allowed and a small head grew heavy on his shoulder. Trust made into weight.

His breath sawed. His body wanted to kneel but he would not kneel to the Council. Not anymore. He knelt to this.

Parrott's voice returned, *When it breaks, follow this.*

It was not the city that had to break first. Not the ledgers. Not even the net of cameras that watched pulses like wolves watch flanks. The first fracture was here, in the mind they had taken and laundered and rung dry. Memory had to split its casing. Love had to kick down the door.

Alice was the foot that did it. The beads in his sleeve were the hinge torn free.

The rain ran warmer down his face. He tasted salt and laughed a small, cracked laugh of his own.

The years between

Memory did not stop at the lip of the kitchen table or the boundary of a field. It pulled back further, as if the mind, once cracked, would not spare anyone.

Between 2026 and 2028, the world surrendered by

increments and insisted it had chosen. Papers said compassion. Podiums said safety. The United Nations gave the future a list and a logo. Governments gave it a password and a price.

Digital ID made obedience visible. First a QR code on a screen that warmed the hand. Then an App on a phone. Then a wearable. Then something that warmed the skin from inside. It was sold as kindness. It mapped as chains.

The names changed with the flags: *Citizen Ledger. Wellbeing Pass. Climate Card. Safety Credit.*

But the permissions did not change. Your right to live became a function of your willingness to be measured.

Question climate change alarmism? Amber. Express a love for borders, for hearth, for the old ways? Red. Say the words *mother* and *father* as if they still meant something particular? Redder still. Refuse a needle? Arrest.

The cleverness did not end with digital data. The face became the key you could not lose. Cameras memorised you. Algorithms learned your tremors. A long blink became intent. A skipped word became a threat. *Pre-crime* detection slid into policy with the quiet of oil on stone. Now you could be arrested for the crime of thought.

The world was not always afraid enough to agree. When fear flagged, they fed it. There were wars that arrived like theatre, right on cue. There were sirens that sang of Cyber Walls and Viral Weather. There were headlines like stage directions. And when even that dulled, they pointed upward. *Look there.* Threats without borders. Shadows without bodies. The promise of a common enemy so vast that populations would submit to safety.

The oldest weapons did the newest harm. Schools that had been built for learning were repurposed for forgetting. Books that taught rebellion became contraband. Children raised under Guidance did not ask where yesterday had gone because they were not given the word *yesterday*. Adults were smoothed with chemicals that sanded grief, grit, and inconvenient recollection down to compliance.

Four years. That was the trick of it. Four years was enough to loosen facts like teeth. By 2028, whole populations woke into a morning without history and told themselves it had always been this way because saying otherwise hurt too much.

They outlawed laughter because laughter remembered. They outlawed prayer because prayer revealed God. They outlawed family with a thousand small renamings until the word *sister* sounded like sabotage.

But memory does not live only in the head. It lives in walls that hold warmth, in tables with knife scars, in beads around a child's neck. It lives in the body of a boy who was a brother. It lives in the sky.

That was why they dimmed the stars.

And that was why he was remembering now.

Paper, softened

The rain had worked its way into the fold. George looked down at his fist and opened it. The square sagged, edges blurred, ink bled into the grain. Still, the lines held. This was not Safety Council paper. It did not dissolve when it touched water.

The map was drawn in a hand that had not practised obedience. Angles were wrong. Arrows were enthusiastic. The path did not look like a path. It looked like a choice.

LEFT, then a second *left* scratched over the first as if the writer had argued with themself. A cut across a courtyard that no longer existed. A symbol he did not recognise that his hands, strangely, did. A box. A downward stroke. A circle, not quite closed, with a cross where you might break it.

At the bottom, where ink had pooled and darkened as if the pen had paused there longer than it should, a single word: REMEMBER.

Not an order. An invitation.

"Alice," he said again, and this time the name was a promise.

He slid the softened paper under his robe against his skin and felt the map's damp cool press into the heat of him. The beads he wound twice around his fingers until they bit and would not slip.

He ran.

The thin places

At the edge of Dockside, the city forgot itself. Fences ended two metres before they reached the corner. Signs pointed to buildings that were not there. Scanners blinked to no one.

George moved through the thin places like a man following a scent. The map did not make sense to his eyes, which had been trained to read only what the Council permitted, but his feet seemed to know. *Left, left again, cut across the yard with the cracked bollard, under the duct with the stagger, through the gap that smells like rain and metal and something sweet you cannot name.*

He kept moving.

Every now and then the sky cleared its throat and showed him more stars. The sight hurt and helped. The rain turned thin and needling. He felt both lighter and more real, as if weight and truth were the same.

He knew he was seen. He did not care the way he used to. Let the machines taste his pulse and write their hymns in red and amber. Numbers were only chains, and chains, once cracked, were invitations.

He reached the place, the circle on the map, and put his hand where the cross broke it.

A hatch. Rust had eaten at its edges. He wiped his palm across its face and left a streak the colour of old blood. The handle stuck and then loosened with an awkward wrenching sound.

George checked the sky once more. It offered a fistful of burning points and then drew its shawl of cloud back over its shoulders, as if to hide him.

"Alice," he whispered. "I'm coming." He did not know if the words meant *to you* or *to myself*. He suspected they meant both.

He pulled the hatch.

The city above him breathed the way a thing exhales when a weight is lifted and does not yet know it. The hatch hovered above his head.

It was the threshold of the old stories, the seam between worlds.

Once crossed, no man returns unchanged.

Chapter 12
The Tunnel and the Light

The hatch clanged shut above him, sealing him into the undercity. The sound went on too long, echoing back and forth down the stone throat until it became indistinguishable from the pounding of his own blood. George stood still, listening, certain the noise would betray him.

The air was different down here. Damp, stale, metallic. He could taste rust and the residue of machines long since buried. Each breath felt heavy, as if it carried dust from a forgotten age.

He moved. Slowly at first, then faster, then slower again as fear seized him in waves. His boots splashed in shallow water. The noise was unbearable. He imagined the authorities triangulating his position by sound alone, drones slithering through the passages to flush him out like vermin.

The tunnels were old, older even than the fifteen-minute cities. Tiles flaked from the walls, exposing concrete eaten by damp. Pipes sagged, dripping in steady rhythms that echoed like clock ticks. Signs, rusted and half-rotted, pointed toward places that no longer existed. It looked less like an engineered passage than a wound the city had hidden and then forgotten.

His thoughts ran in circles, doubt, dread, defiance. And beneath them all, the sharp ache of absence. Alice. He could not summon her face yet, only the hollow where it should have been. Was she alive? Was she erased? The thought hollowed him out further than fear ever could.

He stumbled, pressing a hand to the wall to steady himself. The surface was slick and cold. It thrummed faintly, as though alive. Static crawled into his skull, fragments of voices seeping through, numbers, warnings, commands. None lasted long enough to hold. They passed through him like ghosts.

He moved again. The tunnel stretched endlessly, the ceiling lowering, the air thickening. Every few steps he thought he heard boots behind him, metal scraping, breath that wasn't his. He forced himself not to look back.

Then, faint at first, a glow. A smear of light where no light should be. He froze, chest tight. It might be the others, or it might be the end.

The glow did not fade. Slowly, he began to walk toward it. Each step was heavier than the last. The water rose to his ankles. His movement sounded too loud, as though magnified by the tunnel itself.

Then came the voice.

"George."

He stopped dead. His body seized. The sound was soft, human, not mechanical.

"George. This way."

Erika.

He wanted to believe it, but the tunnels were deceiving, voices stitched from fragments, whispers conjured from the lattice. Yet this one cut straight through. Against his better judgement, he ran. Boots splashing, lungs tearing, the light swelling until it was all he could see.

At the end of the passage, a figure waited. She reached out and pulled him through the doorway before he could think. Her face, pale in the glow, was sharper now, eyes hard, hair damp from the underground air. She looked at him intently.

What George saw before him swallowed him whole.

It was vast, carved deep into the earth, filled with a machine so large it seemed to hold the walls apart. Towers of circuitry rose like pillars. Wires sprawled across the floor and ceiling, disappearing into stone like roots into soil. Screens blinked and scrolled with green and white code. Data cascading too fast for the eye to follow. The air vibrated with the low, ceaseless hum of power.

And standing at its base was Parrott.

He turned slowly, his face lit by the glow. For once, Parrott did not look menacing. His eyes shone with a feverish intensity George had never seen before.

"We have direct communication," Parrott said. His voice was steady, almost reverent. "Not fragments. Not echoes. Not static. Direct." He looked at George. "With the old world dissidents. With the past"

George's breath caught. His throat felt raw. He stared at the machine, then at Erika, who remained silent, watching him with unreadable eyes.

The machine shuddered. Screens flickered, stuttered, then steadied. Words scrawled themselves across the panes in jagged green lines.

George stared, chest tight, but Erika stepped closer. Her voice was low, almost reverent.

"George, it has to be you. You need to input the data. You're the one who has to sit at that console and drive this."

His eyes snapped to hers. "Me? I don't know anything about this. I only know Safety Council code and systems."

"You will," she said, cutting across his panic with calm certainty. "When the time comes, you will."

"There must be someone else to do this," George insisted. His voice cracked under the weight of it. "I know nothing about this system."

Parrott's voice rose, fierce, urgent. "It's you, George. This isn't just transmission. It's communication. The signal on the other end, George, it's not a Council trace. It's an AI node from before the blackout. A dissident hacker from the old world. Someone who broke their systems from the inside."

George shook his head. "And what does that have to do with me?"

Parrott's eyes burned. He took a step closer, voice trembling now, not with doubt but with awe. "It's you, George. Don't you see? You're the one they've been reaching for. The messages, the fragments in the walls. The signal has been trying to get through to *you*. The hacker is you."

The words seemed to split the air itself. George staggered back as if struck, the hum of the machine filling the silence that followed.

The machine shuddered. Screens flickered, stuttered,

then steadied. Words scrawled themselves across the panes in jagged green lines.

TRANSMISSION WEAK.
AUDIO IMPOSSIBLE.
TEXT ONLY.

George lowered himself into the chair before the console. His hands hovered uncertainly, then settled on the keys. The desk was cluttered with relics of old tech, switches worn smooth, ports and sockets that no Pod citizen had ever been trained to use. He scanned the data scrolling in columns of green, his eyes moving the way they had a thousand times in the Safety Council's service. This time the gaze was different, detached from obedience, searching for patterns instead of quotas.

Sure enough, the patterns began to surface. Hidden threads. Familiar loops. His pulse quickened as his mind pulled at the seams. Memory did not rush him all at once; it bled back in fragments.

For a moment, he saw himself at seventeen. Not in a Pod, but hunched before a glowing screen. Fingers flying. Shadows of others beside him, young and defiant, faces half-seen but voices clear.

"You can do it, George," one of them urged, the words threading across years as if no time had passed.

The present snapped back with a jolt. Erika's hand brushed his shoulder. Her voice, steady and insistent, echoed the same line. "You can do it, George. You can remember."

In that instant, everything clicked. The patterns were no longer alien. They were his. The keys beneath his hands felt less like tools and more like home.

His breath caught. His lips moved before his mind could stop them. "I remember."

The words unlocked something deep inside. His fingers dropped to the keys and began to punch in data with a speed and certainty that shocked him. Symbols scrolled faster across the screen, the machine responding as if it had been waiting for his touch all along.

George's eyes widened. New words formed, halting but precise.

WE CAN GIVE YOU TWO OPTIONS.

ONE: ACCESS CODE TO EXIT SYSTEM.
ESCAPE WHILE YOU CAN.
TWO: DIVERT ENTIRE GRID TO
TRANSMISSION. SEND THE MESSAGE OUT.

The smell of hot metal thickened. The choice lingered on the screen, blinking like a sentence already passed.

Parrott stepped closer, face lit by the glow. He was trembling, not with fear but with conviction. "This is it. A chance to tell them what really happened. To pass the truth before the Safety Council buries it again."

George's body sagged under the weight of the words. Arrest meant erasure, Recalibration, public correction. He had seen it happen. And worse, the final death, the stripping away of self until nothing remained but compliance. He wanted to live. He wanted, above all, to find his sister. To find Alice.

If they chose the code, they might have a chance.

But the screens blinked again, insistent.

TIME IS LIMITED. CHOOSE.

Parrott's voice was urgent now. "George, if we run, maybe we live a little longer. But if we stay silent, they win again. They erase it all. We have one chance."

Erika's hand brushed his arm. Her eyes locked on his, calm in a way that unsettled him. "George," she said softly, "what you decide here is what you are."

Sweat ran into his eyes. His throat burned. The ache for the old world hollowed him out. Panic choked him. Yet beneath it flickered a shadow of something older, something harder, the fragments he had heard in the static. *We will not be erased.*

The machine thrummed louder.

CHOOSE.

George stood trembling, caught between the terror of discovery and the unbearable pull of defiance.

To live, or to be remembered.

Chapter 13
The Last Ledger

The machine waited like a living thing, its towers breathing light, its cables slack as veins, its screens watching the three of them with a patience that felt like judgement. The tunnels above hummed with distant alarms. Soft at first, then nearer, then soft again, like sirens heard through water. The choice on the screen remained, green and merciless.

WE CAN GIVE YOU TWO OPTIONS.

ONE: ACCESS CODE TO EXIT SYSTEM.
ESCAPE WHILE YOU CAN.
TWO: DIVERT ENTIRE GRID TO
TRANSMISSION. SEND THE MESSAGE OUT.

Time thinned. The air tasted like coins.

George's hand hovered over the console as if warming itself by a fire. "If we run," he said, "we become ghosts. If we send, we become witnesses."

He couldn't pull his eyes from the words. His pulse fluttered in his throat. His body wanted the first option with the animal clarity of a creature trapped in a snare. Live. Find Alice. Find a corner of the world which the Safety Council has not charted. There must be a place. There had to be.

Erika did not look at the screen. She looked at him. It was the stillness of her gaze that frightened him, the way it refused to bargain. "They trained you to call fear prudence," she said softly. "They trained you to call obedience kindness. They trained you to call forgetting peace. Is it?"

The machine thrummed harder, the lights along its spine climbing toward white.

CHOOSE.

George shut his eyes. The words on the screen burned there anyway. Orbiting them, a constellation of slogans he had heard his whole life:

Harmony is happiness. Safety is mercy. Don't be selfish.

He had mouthed those lines until they wore grooves in his brain. They rose now like a litany at his own trial.

Another litany pushed back in his mind, quieter, older, the fragments of a father's teasing voice, a mother's warm laughter, a child's shriek at the sea. They were no less real for being faint. They were more real for having survived.

A single syllable floated up from the silt of his memory and came to rest on his tongue, "Remember."

The syllable tasted like flint.

He opened his eyes. "We send."

Parrott's shoulders sagged as if he had been holding his breath for years. The fever in him cooled into something like peace. Erika's hand closed, once, over George's knuckles and then withdrew. No speech. No praise. The machine had no use for either.

Fingers flew across the battered keys with grace. The screens split and unfurled like blinds in a storm, lines of code rattling down, windows opening into other windows. Erika pulled a heavy lever rimed with dust, one of the old-world switches that did not care about touch or voice or face, only force. Something groaned deep in the floor, as if the city itself had shifted its weight.

On the main pane, the options vanished.

DIVERT SEQUENCE PRIMED.
WARNING: GRID LOAD CRITICAL.
WARNING: AUDITORS ALERTED.
WARNING: INTERCEPTION.

George's mouth was dry. He could see it all. How the Safety Council had built the world like a problem in arithmetic. Scores, quotas, tolerances, permissible ranges. Even memory had a number now. But what they could not number, they could not own.

"Two streams," Parrott murmured, almost to himself. "Forward to now. Back to then."

George blinked. "Back?"

Parrott nodded, eyes on the code. "You felt it too.

The lattice isn't just listening to walls. It's listening to time. The old frequencies are still alive in the stone. If we hit the angles, if we force the load"

Erika's voice cut across the hum. "We don't have the angles. But we have the will."

She looked at George again. "Are you ready to be what you believe?"

A question. Not a slogan. It broke something in him and set something else alight.

He stepped to the final switch. It was fat with years of dust, its rubber collar cracked, its metal throat dark. He thought of his sister, the warmth of a small hand, the cadence names his lungs tried on and could not keep. He thought of Erika's face on the day in the cocooned room when the machine breathed with his breath. He thought of fields and fire and hymns. He thought of the world as it might be if the laughter they had heard in the walls became free again.

Above them, a new sound entered the cavern. Not alarms now, but something quicker and colder. The hiss of drones in a vent. The distant bite of boots finding the rhythm of a hunt.

"We're out of minutes," Parrott said. It was not fear. It was fact.

George wrapped his fingers around the switch.

The Choice That Cannot Be Erased

You have been told all your life that choices are private. That they belong to you. That your courage or your cowardice ends at the skin. This is a lie that flatters you into inaction.

Some choices reverberate.

Some choices wake nations.

Some choices crack time.

Here is one of them.

When you are promised an exit, when your body begs for a door, when the world is built to make bravery feel like suicide, do you stand? Or do you sit back and witness? Do you give the tyrants what they demand? Or do you give your soul what it is owed?

They teach you to call standing up 'dangerous'. They teach you to call surrender 'care'. They teach you to call the shuttering of your mind 'kindness'. Be precise now. Name things as they are. Fear is the instrument. Silence is the cage. Compliance is the noose.

What would you do?

The Moment of No Return

He threw the switch.

The cavern answered like a struck bell. For a second there was no sound, only pressure, as if the air had become something you could lean against. Then the grid took the weight.

Light tore through the machine. It didn't climb or fall; it expanded, as if the device had become a lung and the city had exhaled into it. Every dark seam along the walls lit up with a thin streak of white. The screens filled not with numbers but with words. Ragged at first and then steady. They were not the Safety Council's words.

A mother soothing a baby.

A father bellowing with laughter.

A child calling out to a friend.

A table laid. Bread broken. Grace said.

A flag raised.

A nation standing proud.

A people celebrating their heritage, their history, their voices.

The sounds and images poured from the machine into the tunnels and into the feed lines that ran like rivers beneath the Pods. George felt them moving. Not just in his ears. In the stone. In the water. In the dust. The city had been engineered to a paste of neutral tones; suddenly colour bled underneath it, as if the map of the world had remembered its own buried hues.

"Forward stream holding," Parrott said, eyes wide, voice tight with wonder. "Pods receiving. Every wall that listens is hearing."

"The back stream?" Erika asked.

Parrott's fingers chattered. "It's… it's not a stream,

it's a scatter. The old grid isn't a grid at all." His mouth twitched into a grin that was nothing like his daily chirp. "This is you George"

On a second pane, dates that had not been used in years flickered alive. 2026 winked through static, vanished, returned as if embarrassed by being seen. The machine found a seam and drove the sound through. Voice without audio, music without notes, what the walls knew passed as text, then as pulse, then as impression. Somewhere, in a year that still believed it would be spared, someone reached to turn off a radio and found their hand had paused.

George's palm burned. He looked down and realised he had been gripping the beads so tightly the colours had imprinted his skin. He loosened his fingers. The imprint remained, a child's bracelet translated onto a man's flesh.

The drones were closer now. Erika was already moving. She pulled a drawer from under the console and revealed a narrow passage. She shoved a pack into Parrott's chest. "Door two. As rehearsed. North stair."

Parrott hesitated, just long enough to be human. "What about…"

"I'll take him," she said.

He searched George's face and the tinny fervour that had always annoyed George became something like love. Parrott put his forehead to George's for a heartbeat. A gesture from some older ritual, and then he was gone. All elbows and conviction, vanishing into the seam with the grace of a man who would never again chirp about Guidance.

Erika looked at George. "If they take me," she said, "you don't wait."

"If they take me," he began, but she shook her head once, and the shake was a sentence.

"Look," she said.

On the main screen the words had changed. No longer the scenes of kitchens and fields. A single line had written itself in the middle of the pane, as though the machine had tired of voices and wanted something that could be carved.

SOMEONE MUST ALWAYS REMEMBER.

The line brightened and duplicated, sheeted across subsidiary panes until the cavern seemed filled with that one sentence. It did not shout. It did not plead. It simply held.

Erika's hand found his again, and this time she did not let go. "They're coming," she said.

They moved along a corridor of cables toward a door cut into the rock and braced by steel. The machine kept singing in words. George felt a curl of pride that had nothing to do with himself. It felt like being part of a courage that did not need his name.

In the passage beyond the door, the air chilled. A gust rattled the lamps. Above, faster now, the boots had found a pattern the stone could not disguise. The Council hated noise; it had taught the city to wear soft shoes. Footsteps that were loud meant haste. Haste meant fear. The thought pleased him more than he could comprehend.

At the angle of two tunnels, Erika stopped. A panel lifted like a held breath released. Behind it, a shaft climbing impossibly narrow, studded with old metal rungs. She nodded at it. "Up," she said.

"What about you?" His voice came rough.

"I'll slow them," she said.

"No," he relied. "We go together."

"We will," Erika breathed, and he recognised the trick and the love inside it at the same time.

He wanted to argue, to take the heroic sentence back from the machine and spend it here on anger. But the words on the screen had been correct. Courage was not a performance. It was a debt paid in the dark. He took the first rung.

A sound cut the air. Not a siren. A voice. The Guidance had found a way into the tunnels. The neutral genderless warmth fell from a grille like oil.

"Citizens," it cooed, "please remain calm. A safety anomaly is being corrected. Witnessing is harmful. Forgetting is peace."

Erika's laugh startled him. It was low and almost

kind. "They're always late," she said. She pointed up. "Go."

He climbed. His hands slipped on cold iron. He smelled his own fear and something like exhilaration under it. After eight rungs, he looked down. Erika had not moved. Her eyes were on him as if she could climb his spine with her gaze and take his weight.

"Say it," she said.

He didn't ask what. He knew.

"Remember," he called back, and discovered that speaking the word cleared the air a little.

The drones arrived in a line, their lights slicing the passage into segments like butcher's twine. Behind them came three Auditors in the slate robes and blurred faces of the Safety Council, HushWands at their hips, palms already raised to soothe and subdue. Erika stepped into the light as though joining a conversation at a party. The lead Auditor's face saw her and failed to register a category. The pause was very small and very precious.

"Citizen," the Guidance said through small mouths. "You are in error. Return to your Pod. We will assist you"

Erika looked up the shaft a last time. Her face softened in that instant and became almost girlish, not in age but in unarmouredness. "Find her," she said.

The HushWands cracked. The drones tightened their line. Erika moved like water around a rock, a step and a half-step, drawing the line away from the shaft mouth and into the broader throat of the corridor. She did not run. She did not shout. She chose the angle and offered herself as bait.

George climbed until his arms shook and the rungs blurred. The shaft opened into a spill of black that his eyes needed to name before his body could accept. He hauled himself onto a ledge and rolled, panting, into a pocket of stale air. Far below, a voice, not Guidance, rose once. It was Erika's. He could not hear the words. He knew them anyway, *Go.*

He got to his knees. A grille set low to the ground leaked city light in a flat oblong. He pressed his eye to it. He saw, impossibly far away, the evening skin of Dockside, the way the corridor surfaces held the last of the day like memory.

He slid the grille aside and shouldered through.

Hands closed around his wrist.

They were not Erika's. They were not Parrott's. The grip was professional and careful and complete. He was pulled like a fish from water into the corridor and into the wide shadow of an Auditor who had no face at all, only a blur where a face should live.

"Citizen George," the blur said in its warm fog, "correction will not be merciful."

Chapter 14
The Crossroads

They told him forgetting was peace. They told him silence was safety. They told him obedience was mercy.

But George had remembered, and for that, he was here.

Every system writes its own ending. For the World Safety Council, it was silence. For George, it was memory. The two could not live together, and so the last ledger was written in chains.

Because stories do not die in cells. Voices slip through walls. Words spoken in truth outlast the machines that try to erase them. And even here, bound and waiting, George carried that power. The power of story. The power of speech. The power of what is true.

There were no machines now. No pulsing bracelets, no walls breathing with instruction, no soothing voice of Guidance. Only the silence of stone, the echo of his own breath, and the certainty of his end.

George sat alone in the holding cell. His wrists and neck were bare. His eyes unshackled by glass. It felt strange, almost unnatural, to have nothing pressing against his body. Nothing telling him who he was.

The Safety Council had no need of chains now. The sentence itself was enough.

The walls were blank, pale, humming faintly with the absence of colour. He had lived his whole life under the blur of slogans and the haze of sedation. Now, at the final moment, he saw the world as it truly was, bare, stripped of lies, emptied of illusion.

But it was not terror that filled him. It was memory.

He remembered the fields.

Not the sterilised parks of the Pods, with their artificial trees and their clipped, recycled air. No, fields wide and green, grasses moving like waves in the wind, the scent of soil alive and damp after rain. The air had been wild, unpredictable, sharp enough to sting his lungs and fill his chest until it ached.

He remembered the woodlands.

Where shadows stretched long across the paths
and branches formed cathedrals overhead.
He remembered climbing trees as a boy, bark
scratching his hands, resin sticking to his fingers. He
remembered chasing Alice down paths littered with
leaves that crunched and snapped beneath their feet.
She had laughed so hard she had fallen into the moss,
rolling until her cheeks were stained with earth.

He remembered the sea.

A horizon without walls, without quotas, without
permission. Waves breaking endlessly, each one a
kind of freedom, each one telling him that nothing
could ever truly be contained. The salt stung his lips,
his hair whipped in the wind, and Alice had shrieked
with joy when the foam wrapped around her ankles.

He remembered fire.

Not the flicker of screens or the simulated warmth of
Council heating systems, but real fire, logs splitting,

flames leaping, sparks drifting upward into the night. The fire had warmed his hands, his face, his very bones. It had given light to stories, laughter, arguments that stretched into the early hours.

He remembered taste.

Food that was more than fuel. He remembered the sweet burst of fruit still warm from the sun, the richness of bread pulled steaming from the oven, the sharp tang of cheese that caught at the back of his tongue. He remembered meals shared, not rationed, tables that were crowded with plates and voices and love.

He remembered worship.

The sound of hymns rising in a church, voices imperfect yet somehow complete together. He remembered the sense of something greater than himself, something that gave shape to love and sacrifice, something the Safety Council had named superstition but which had once given him strength.

He remembered the land.

England as it once was, rolling green hills rising soft against the horizon, fields quilted with hedgerows, rivers winding like silver threads through valleys. The salt wind off the coast, the clang of church bells on a Sunday, the laughter of children running barefoot through meadows. A place imperfect, fragile, but alive. A place worth saving because it was real.

He remembered freedom.

The simple freedom of walking where he chose, speaking what he thought, holding the hands of the people he loved without glancing over his shoulder. The freedom to imagine a different tomorrow and to work toward it without fear. The freedom to be imperfect, to fail, to fall, to rise again.

And above all, he remembered love.

Love that was not measured in quotas, not filtered through compliance, not conditional on safety. Love that was fierce, unplanned, and alive.

The transmission had gone out. He knew this much.

Across every Pod, every wall, every circuit of the machine, the forbidden voices had poured, a mother soothing a baby, a father teasing his son, a little girl giggling without fear. The new world of the Safety Council had heard the old laughter once again. The old prayers, the old love. For a moment, however brief, citizens who had lived in the blur were shown what had been stolen from them.

What they did with it, whether to bury it again or to rise, George didn't know.

Do nothing, and the Safety Council would tighten its grip. Rise, and the Agenda would fall. The choice no longer belonged to him. It belonged to the millions who sat drugged and dulled, their instincts suppressed, their imaginations outlawed, who might yet stir at the sound of their own forgotten souls.

The transmission had not only been sent forward. It had been sent back. Through the cracks of time, across the fragile threads of memory itself, another signal had gone out.

Not for 2030 but for the old world.

A warning to those who still had time to choose.

Before they came for him, Erika had slipped away. In the dim corridor, she had pressed her hand into his, her eyes fierce with a light that even the Safety Council could not dim. She had told him his sister was safe. That there were still corners of the earth not bound by the net, still places where the Council's hand had not yet reached. She would take her there. She would tell her the truth. She would tell her what her brother had done in the last days of the empire.

George closed his eyes. The silence pressed in, but it was no longer empty. It was filled with the memory of laughter, of love. It was filled with the fire of a spirit that could never be caged, rewritten or erased.

Footsteps echoed in the corridor. The door unlatched.

George rose.

He did not know if the world would wake. He did not know if the Agenda would fall. But he knew that once, for a brief and shining moment, the truth had broken through. And in that moment, he had been free.

And what happens next is no longer his story. It is yours.

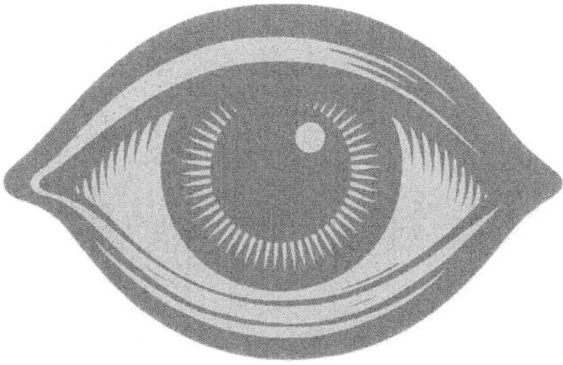

Epilogue

Somewhere, beyond the reach of walls and wires, a child runs through the fields. The grass bends beneath her feet, tall enough to brush against her knees, wildflowers nodding as she passes. Her laughter rises into the open air, unmeasured, unapproved, carried only by the wind. She stumbles, falls, and rolls, the earth smudging her cheeks, the sky vast and unbroken above her.

She knows who she is. Not who she was told she must be, not who the Safety Council insisted she must become. She is a child of God.

Not indoctrinated.
Not filled with fear.
Not told to silence her questions or to swallow her doubts.
Not poisoned with the lie that there is no God, no meaning, no soul.

She is free.

Free to fall, to rise, to wonder.

Free to laugh without permission, to speak without script.

Free to seek truth without being told it is dangerous.

Free to remember that love is not compliance, and faith is not a crime.

Her laughter carries, unbroken.
And somewhere, others are beginning to remember too.

It is also told that a man was seen escaping as the tyranny faltered. A man who refused to forget. Freed by memory, driven by faith, he searches for the family stolen from him. His voice is faint, his signal fragile.

But it is growing.

Every question asked, every lie resisted, every laugh that cannot be silenced makes the signal stronger. The transmission only needs another rebel. Another soul unwilling to bow. Another spark willing to burn.

A dissident voice, a freedom fighter, a fearless rebel.

And perhaps that person is you.

About the Author

Mike Fairclough is an internationally acclaimed educator with thirty years' experience in the field, including nineteen years as a high-profile headmaster. He has been at the forefront of character education in Britain, focusing on risk-taking, the building of resilience, and outdoor learning. He has received widespread media attention for his approach, including teaching children to fire shotguns, skin rabbits, and to cook over an open fire.

Fairclough was the only serving headteacher or school principal, out of 43,500 in the United Kingdom, to publicly question the Covid 'vaccine' rollout to children.

He is the author of six books, Playing With Fire, Wild Thing, Rewilding Childhood, Take Daily, The Hero's Voice and Cancel THIS. He is ghostwriter and editor for Kevin Anderson and Associates, a leading firm, trusted by New York Times bestselling authors, CEOs, and thought leaders, to bring their stories and ideas to life. Mike is also an editor for Fisher King Publishing, supporting outspoken authors and their works and their right to free speech.

Also by Mike Fairclough

Cancel THIS

A response to the Orwellian levels of
censorship within modern Britain

The Hero's Voice

Finding the courage to speak out

Playing with Fire

Embracing risk and danger in schools

Wild Thing

Embracing Childhood Traits in Adulthood
for a Happier, More Carefree Life

Rewilding Childhood

Raising Resilient Children Who Are
Adventurous, Imaginative and Free

Printed in Dunstable, United Kingdom